D.D. Watson

Puppet's Lesson

Pet Sitting Book 3

Hardcore Submission Erotica

About the Publisher
4Fun Publishing, a member of **BLVNP Incorporated**, 340 S. Lemon #6200, Walnut CA 91789, info@blvnp.com / legal@blvnp.com
NOTE: Due to the highly emotional reaction of some people to works of erotic fiction, any email sent to the above address that contains foul language or religious references is automatically deleted by our anti-spam software and will not be seen. All other communications are welcome.

DISCLAIMER
Please don't be stupid and kill yourself. This book is a work of FICTION. Do not try any new sexual practice that you find in this book. It is fiction and not to be confused with reality. Neither the author nor the publisher or its associates assume any responsibility for any loss, injury, death or legal consequences resulting from acting on the contents in this book. Every character in this book is over 18 years of age. The author's opinions are not to be construed as the opinions of the publisher. The material in this book is for entertainment purposes ONLY. Enjoy.

Pet Sitting, Book 3

Puppet's Lesson

Hardcore Submission Erotica

D. D. Watson

© **D. D. Watson 2014**
ISBN: 978-1-62761-837-3

PUPPET moved freely through the house she shared with her Master, Troy Utter. When he was at his office in the city, Puppet was allowed to do as she pleased when he was away, provided she did her online schooling to gain her college degree and to remain bare skin and to wear her collar. Neither posed a problem to Puppet as her chosen classes were her first choices, and she would rather wander around in the nude.

While she sat in the kitchen, eating grapes by the large panel on the window on a bright sunny day; Puppet stretched out on her back on a cushioned bench with her legs crossed, bobbing her leg up and down as she peels each grape before she devoured it. Her exposition was witnessed by the hired gardener, who was 10 years her Master's senior; and his two employees, one younger male and female who were about Puppet's age. They came every week to make sure the garden, that was also Puppet's play area, was well cared for. High soft shrubs aligned the borders of the enclosed play area that was Puppet's; behind that was a concrete wall that circled the area and covering that were creeping vines that overtook the wall giving the illusion of solitude.

Though Troy Utter's property was vast, he employed trusted workers to create an oasis for her within the grounds, a fountain that he filled with exotic goldfish that were Puppet's favorite. All this was attached to his home, so her pet door only went into her play area. Normally Puppet would be working on her studies or sleeping in when the gardeners arrived, but that morning the warm sun touched her skin and eased her up and out of bed to seize the day with mischief on her mind.

Every morning, a bowl of fresh fruit was placed in her room along with her breakfast that was always warm and delicious whenever she was ready to eat it. She chose to ignore the hot food and glanced out her window that overlooked her play area and saw an older man who was in great shape considering his age, carrying two large brown sacks, one on each shoulder towards the tall shrubs. He stacked them one on top of the other as he wiped his forehead. Then, as if he knew she was watching, he turned and looked up at her. Puppet never met him before but her Master trusts him.

He waved to her and not to be rude, she waved back. His attention turned to something else and Puppet looked and noticed a young male walking up to him. They exchanged a few words then the older man leaned down and kissed the other male on the lips. She could see their hands touching the other's chest and arm. The kiss was deep and watchable as Puppet for once enjoyed the display of passion below her.

They parted and laughed, a small, shy lover's laugh as they both walked off together. Puppet wanted to see more, so she took her grapes downstairs and the gardeners were granted Puppet's appearance and got an eyeful of the beautiful pet as she sat on the floor by the tall French windows with her fruit.

Puppet was well aware of the eyes watching her and delighted in it; she used to avoid eyes that her Master didn't approve, but the gardener and her Master were well acquainted, so he knew about her and her Master's relationship. Of course, he was a bit taken back when she appeared at the window leading to her play area, but told his workers to keep working as he walked out of view retrieving his cellphone.

Puppet didn't want them to ignore her so she began to give them a show as she'd rolled on her side and onto her stomach on the chilled floor, they got a full picture of her physique. She noticed the female, who was about her age, wearing worn jeans and t-shirt that was ripped just above her right C-cup breast. Puppet wanted to rip it further and suck the sweaty tit until the girl went mad with lust and finger fuck her with her rough and callused hands; Puppet's fantasy got the better of her as her own fingers moved towards her wet shaved cunt, spreading her legs so the girl could watch her burlesque show.

She had just started to feel the wetness when the house phone rang. Her head spun and she sprinted for the phone catching it on the second ring.

"Utter's residence," she said.

"Puppet," said her Master dispassionately.

"Hello, Master, how are you?"

"Quiet, Puppet! I received a call that you were distracting the gardeners."

"No..."

"Don't lie to me," he said with a bite in his voice.

"Yes, Master. Sorry, Master."

"You will be. Now listen, my driver is coming for you to bring you to me. Be ready and out the door once he arrives, understood?"

"Yes, Master."

"Wear something simple, you won't be wearing it long and stay your arse upstairs until he comes." The line disconnected before Puppet had a chance to reply.

She left her grapes and the gardeners and hurried upstairs in fear the driver would arrive any moment. He's done that before and her Master punished her for not moving faster.

Outside, the older man pocketed his cell and returned to his duties as he glanced and saw the girl licking her parched lips and drained a bottle of water.

Troy's driver arrived an hour later and Puppet was dressed wearing only a faded tee, no bra, yoga pants, no panties and simple sneakers with no socks. She had the cell that her Master gave her in her pocket, ready to go as instructed, with her collar and latch in hand.

The driver honked once as she exits the house closing the door tightly behind her. The driver opened the back passenger door for her and drove her to her engagement.

When they reached the house, which was ranc-style, she felt a bit anxious on the matter of lying to her Master; the driver helped her out of the car and told her that Mr. Utter wanted her to enter without knocking. Then he climbed back into the car and drove away.

Puppet walked up the path and entered through one of the double doors and disrobed as always and fastened the so familiar collar on her long neck and latched her leash on the catch, then placed her leash between her teeth, and on hands and knees she crawled into the next room to greet her Master.

But to Puppet's surprise she didn't find him on the couch; in his place instead was a folded piece of paper with the word "pet" on it. She took it from its resting place and opened it.

It was a written note telling her to remain on her knees and to go out to the pool.

This new house did have a patio and with closer inspection through the window, she did see the pool but was too petrified to venture outside.

Her cellphone rang startling her. She knew it was her Master calling and she didn't want to keep him waiting. She rushed to her clothes and dug the small phone out of her pocket but was only able to answer it on the fourth ring. She said hello, first there was silence, then the voice was clear as ice.

"You fucking whore!"

"Yes, Master?'

"Crawl that ass out here now!"

"B-but…."

"Excuse me!"

"Nothing, Master, I'm coming."

"You have five seconds!"

The line went dead. She dropped the cell and hurried on hands and knees out to the pool.

There he was, her Master stretched out on a lounge chair on his stomach with not a stitch of clothing on. His perfect ass already tanned in the hot sun. He'll have a beautiful all-over tan by tomorrow. Puppet crawled over beside him. He didn't look at her, his eyes were turned away, sitting back on her hind legs with the leash returned to her painted mouth.

He turned to her and stood up, his cock and balls just a few inches from her face.

"So, you know how to swim, cunt?" he asked, looking down at her, snatching her leash from her mouth and unlatching it from the collar, not caring that he was jerking her neck uncomfortably.

"No, Sir," she said, with tension in her voice.

"It's time you did." He grabbed her forearms and pulled her to stand, he turns her back to his and bounds her wrists with the leather leash making sure she could not free herself.

She's spun back and forced back to her knees. He grabs hold of the studded collar, which he purchased for her when they first agreed to be Master and pet. He found it in an accommodating shop in town, where he became a frequent visitor. His knuckles pressed into her neck as he pulled her face towards his cock, grabbing the back of her head he pushed Puppet's face into his firm muscle holding it there. Her air was locked off, only the scent of his heat filtered through her nostrils.

"Now, cunt, you're going to do breathing exercises. I want you to hold your breath for one minute if you can do this I'll give you a kiss, if you can hold it for two minutes I'll fuck you and for three minutes I'll let you skip this whole lesson."

He pulled her face away allowing his pet to catch her breath.

"Ready, set, go." He returned her face to his crotch and counted to himself.

Puppet tried to hold out but she was failing her task. She began to struggle as she rocked her head from side to side trying to find air until he became fed up with her skirmish and pushed her to the hard ground.

"Pathetic, you couldn't even do a minute. What is it cunt, you don't like my kisses?"

"Yes, Master, I love them."

"Then you should have tried harder."

"Yes, Master. I'm sorry, Master, I'll do better."

"This is going to cost you, cunt."

"Yes, Master."

"SHUT UP!"

Silence.

"Four points. Now let's move on, this will cost you six points if you fail, cunt. But if you pass, I'll deduct three of the points you already have."

Troy left Puppet and walked towards a table that had a medium-sized box on it, he dug through it and seemed please to find what he was looking for. Puppet, still with her hands bound, kept busy by staring at her Master's well-defined body as it glistened with sweat. Her mouth watered as he took no care to cover his cock as it bounced along with his balls. How she wanted to taste those balls and feast on that cock until it came back to life, draining the seed from it, hearing him moan with pleasure until it slipped from her lips.

Her thoughts took her to a fantasy that prevented her from seeing Troy approaching and slapping her across the face, bring her back to reality in a rush. Puppet's head spun as she blinked the dizziness away and felt the burning sting of her Master's palm on her cheek. She licked her lips as if he gave her something sweet to eat.

"Stop day dreaming, whore, and listen, because I am only going to explain this once."

She looked up at him, still shaken from the strike but alert.

"I want you to blow this ball up in 30 seconds, can you do that?"

"Yes, Master."

"Good."

He untied her wrists.

"Stand up," he said, she obeyed and he handed the flat plastic ball to her, standing behind her. "Spread your legs." Again she obeyed. "Now when I say go, you start; not before, understood?"

"Yes, Master."

"Good. I will be counting softly in your ear and at the same time fingering your ass and cunt and maybe your tits. Understood?"

"Y-yes Master."

He placed his hands on her hips and moved close to her ear.

"On the count of three," he said.

Puppet felt the fingers on his right hand move between her legs, passed her first lip and rested against her clit.

"One." Then his fingers on his left hand traveled between her buttocks, resting just at the entrance of her ass hole.

"Two."

Puppet rose the dead ball to her lips trying not to think about the pleasure that was about to erupt. "Three."

Puppet attacked her task as fast as she could and so did he. She almost fell over from his touch alone. He kept her position as he pinched and pulled at the clit and pushed two of his digits into her tight hole. She was dizzy from the invasion but wanted to win his challenge.

"…ten, eleven, twelve, thirteen…"

His counting in her ear was deep hot breaths followed by the tip of his tongue licking her earlobe or his teeth biting it. Luscious rhythm of heat raced through her body and she wasn't even half way.

"…twenty, twenty-one, twenty-two…"

Puppet tried to block his power by blowing harder and felt she was going to win this challenge when he changed tactics. First it was two fingers than he wedged three, forcing their way inside her tight passage. It was heaven as her mouth slipped from the nozzle.

"…twenty-seven, twenty-eight, twenty-nine, thirty."

He took the ball from her and pushed her to the ground. Thankfully, with her hands free, she was able to stop her face from hitting the hard surface.

He tested the firmness of the ball and found it wasn't as complete as it should have been.

"That's six points, cunt, added to what?"

Puppet thought for a minute and luckily remembered.

"Four, Master."

"And what is the total whore?"

"Ten, Master?" she questioned it, why did she do that? She could see him narrowing his eyes towards her.

"Don't you know you stupid, cunt?"

"Ten, Master, it's ten," she said, sounding reassured.

"Now for being stupid, it's twelve. One point for daydreaming and one for responding to me with a question."

He kicked her and reattached her leash dragging her towards the pool.

"Time to get wet, get in pet."

Puppet feared the thought of getting into the pool but didn't wanting to anger her Master, so she slowly eased herself into the tempered water, but was too slow for her Master's taste, so he gave her a shove. As the water circled over her head, she desperately felt for the side of the pool and found her bearings when her feet touched the floor of the pool. Even though the water came to her chest, she trembled and wanted to get out.

Her Master climbed in next to her and without a word or care for her apparent fear, he tugged on her leash and walked her away from the safety of the wall to where the water only touched his upper chest but it touched her neck. Puppet wanted to cry but remembered he promised nothing bad will happen to her.

He turned and placed his hands on her still shaking shoulders.

"Stay, don't you dare follow me out or return to the wall, understood?"

"Yes, Master," she said meekly. He launched his body towards the deeper end of the pool diving under and not emerging until he reached the ladder. He climbed out and went back to the box. He was only there for a second to obtain a mesh bag that held something bright yellow; he returned to the water diving under again and this time emerging beside his pet. His sudden appearance caused the water to buckle, she had to stand on her toes so not to taste the water. He stood watching her, his face and hair dripping of water; how she wanted to drink each drop.

He grabbed hold of her collar and pulled her towards him. He started to lean down towards her lips, as all of Puppet's hopes swelled, he pulled away and spun her around so that her back was to him. If it weren't for him holding her shoulders, she would have slipped on the tiles below and went under. He leaned in close to her ear.

"You still need to earn my kisses, dog," he held up the bag. "See this? We're going to play fetch, each one you return to me earns you a kiss or a point off your…how many points do you have, dog?"

"Twelve, Master."

"Correct. Now back to the wall." He gave her a push as she struggled to get to the wall fast, he was already there sitting on the side. He opened the bag and showed Puppet he had ten yellow plastic dog bones. "Now, dog, tell me the rules."

"Each one I bring back to you, I can either get a kiss or a point taken off my twelve points."

"Correct, now if you can't retrieve one you, get two more points, added to you score. You may not climb out of the pool until the game is over, no rewards are given until the game is over, understood?"

"Yes, Master."

"Also, you can only return the bone between your teeth, understood?"

"Yes, Master."

He pulled out one bone and held it up, and being an obedient pet, she held her gaze on the object ready to follow and fetch it as quickly as she could.

"Ready, set, go." He tossed it and she hurried to retrieve it but realized that as she makes waves, the bone floated towards the deeper end of the pool; she tried to chase it but it was too late, it got away from her. She turned to her Master in shame.

"Two, points," he just said then picked out another and tossed it. This time she was in front of it and was able to fetch it between her teeth and return it to her Master. He let her drop it into his hand.

He raised the next one and tossed it. She took care to move slower towards it, but it still tried to float away, but she caught it and placed it between her teeth and carried it back, dropping it into her Master's hand.

The fourth one was sent flying, and she went with caution to retrieve it but it floated farther away than the last and she lost it. She waited for the next one, and he tossed it and once again she was in front of it, so it was easier to find. He sent the next one and she was making better effort of retrieving it again, placing it between her teeth and instead of dropping it into her Master's hand, she placed it.

He took no notice to it and tossed another one; she went to get it, but must have been overly confident because she forgot to watch her footing and slipped into the deeper end of the pool. All she could see was water and couldn't hear anything. Panic gripped her but then she felt someone grab her arm and pulled her to the surface. She was at the wall gasping for air and holding on for dear life then she heard his voice, telling her to relax, as he rubbed her back and held her close.

"You're fine now, Puppet." She found comfort in his arms as he turned her around and hugged her. "Are you all right?" She nodded into his chest, feeling stupid as tears escaped her eyes.

"Why are you crying?"

"It scared me, Master."

"But you're safe now and with me, didn't you believe me when I told you I'd protect you?'

"Yes, Master."

"Good, now you have three more to go. Tell me when you're ready." He moved from her and resumed his former position sitting on the edge of the pool while Puppet swallowed her fear, knowing her Master did not like to wait. She moved away from the wall and waited for her Master to throw another. He tossed it and slowly she went for it, it wasn't anywhere near the deeper end but her fear took the best of her as she turned back to the wall, not able to look at her Master.

"If you stop playing, the remaining pieces will be points against you, and I promise I will not hold back."

The fear of his wrath was more terrifying than the water. She turned and moved slowly towards the bone and caught it and placed it between her teeth and carried it back. He accepted it and caressed her cheek with his thumb.

"Good, dog."

The eighth one was thrown, and again she was able to retrieve it. The last one was tossed, but it got away from her, thus, ending the game.

Her Master allowed her to climb out of the pool. He climbed out after and walked her inside to the bathroom where he turned on the water and adjusted the temperature. He removed her collar and leash and nudged her into the shower, entering with her.

Under the jet sprays, Puppet couldn't stop shaking as she felt her Master move in behind her. The shower could well accommodate four people, but her Master stood exceedingly close to her as he reached around her, almost like a hug, and took a liquid soap off the shelf and poured it onto a sponge, which was hanging on a hook nearby. Once the desired amount of soap met his approval, he held it under the cascading water and fisted the sponge, releasing the multitude of suds that ran down his arm.

He held Puppet still with a hand on her shoulder as he proceeded to scrub her, starting from her neck, along her shoulders, down both her arms, across her belly, and with slow but strong hands, he caressed her healthy breast keeping close attention on her hard nipples. The sponge passed over them again and again bending and taunting them. Occasionally, his fingers grazed the rigid flesh sending sparks through Puppet's nerve ends.

"There now, you're not shaking anymore. Starting to feel better?" he asked with concern in his voice.

"Yes, Master. Thank you, Master."

"Good…" he dropped the sponge and stepped away from her. "Now you can wash me and finish yourself."

Puppet was surprised that the pampering had stopped but collected herself, and stooped down to retrieve the sponge. She rose and turned to her Master, who stood with his arms by his side, waiting.

At first she wasn't sure where to begin, so instead of asking, she took the cue from her Master and started from his neck.

Thicker than hers, she cleaned it with care as she did his sturdy shoulders and long muscular arms. She moved the sponge to his chest and she placed she placed her free hand on one of his triceps, as she moved her hand in circular motions across his prevailing chest and hard nipples.

She dropped the loofa towards his well-defined six-pack and pressed in hard, as she felt each of his ripple through the soft surface. As she continued to his crotch, her Master seized both her wrists and made her hold the sponge in both hands as he lowered them and scrub his privates. Both hands grasped around his cock and stroked the semi erect muscle to full stance. Then he made her wash his balls in the same manner, building the suds as she squeezed and lather between his legs. Once he was satisfied with her work, he released her wrists.

"Finish the rest of my body, dog, and don't take forever," he said, dropping his arms back to his side. Puppet hurried to comply soaping both legs and feet before standing.

He made her switch places with him.

"Finish cleaning yourself before I finish rinsing off or I'll give you another five points."

Puppet didn't want that so she quickly lathered her legs and feet, then saturated her shaved pussy and ass as quickly as she could, all the while watching the water drive the suds off her Master's body.

He stepped from under the water when he was sure the soap was off and out the shower.

"Don't keep me waiting, Puppet; rinse off and get out here." Wrapping his soaked body in a towel, he left the bathroom. Puppet darted under the water and used her hands to push off the soap as she felt the temperature turn from warm to cold rather quickly. He had the shower on a timer, just like home, she suspected. As her body shivered again but not from fear, but from the icy blast she had to endure while still rinsing her privates. Stepping back, she turned the water off and carefully stepped out of the shower and grabbed a big warm towel that was waiting for her.

"Puppet, I want you out here drying off, now," he barked and Puppet jumped as she hurried to fulfill his demand. She stopped when she saw him with his back to her, bent over while drying his muscular calf. His ass cheeks spread apart, exposing his hair line that shelled his forbidden entrance. That once every so often, her Master would grant her play time to explore his velvet slit with her tongue and sometimes fingers.

Oh, how he moaned and rocked his ass to gain deeper penetration from her skilled mouth and fingers. Puppet took care to run the towel over her damp body as her fantasy about submitting to her Master's desires took full flight in her mind.

She sat on the floor and dried her feet, as she continued to watch her Master finish his own drying and folded his towel, draping it on the back of a chair.

He turned his attention to Puppet, walking over to her and taking her towel and tossing it aside.

"Stand up. I want to make sure you did a good job." Puppet rose to her feet and placed her hands behind her head as her Master studied every inch of her body, from her neck, to her breast; he lifted and squeezed each one; along her spine, spreading her ass checks, then taking her to the bed. He made her lay her torso on the soft surface while he kneeled down and examined her arse hole and wet pussy. His fingers parted the lips as he entered and explored her clit. When he was satisfied, he made her stand.

"Hands at your side." He refastened her collar and leash and had Puppet kneel on the floor in front of him as he sat on the bed.

"Let's see, you retrieved six bones but lost four. The four toys added to your score is what, dog?"

"Twenty, Master."

"Correct. Now you have six bones you could use them to deduct six points from your score or buy six kisses. What do you want to do?"

"Deduct five points from my score and buy a kiss, Master."

"Sounds wise. Done. When would you like your kiss, now or later?"

"Now, Master."

"You can have it in any way or anywhere you want, just tell me."

"Lying down on the bed, with you on top of me, full kiss, and I want to hold you...Master."

"Very well, one full kiss lying down and you may hold me."

He rose and pulled her leash for her to stand and walked her over to the bed. She lay on her back in the middle as he crawled on top of her. She wrapped her arms around his neck and pulled him into a kiss. Their tongues twitched back and forward in each other's mouth, her hands combing through his raven pepper hair, forcing his mouth closer.

She felt his hands fondling her tits and pulling her hair, but mostly his cock growing big and firm against her body. Then, as quickly as the kiss started, it stopped. Her Master drew away from her and climbed off the bed. He was panting but quickly regained control. As he walked to a side table and opened the bottom drawer, he spoke to her.

"Time for you to pay back your points, dog. Roll over onto your stomach and spread your arms and legs out." She obeyed as he rose, holding the bindings. All four of her joints were tied to the bed and a blindfold was placed over her eyes.

The wait was short when she felt the hard leather connect with her butt cheek. She cried out but was cut short when another blow was struck again and again, she was whipped repeatedly. Her pleas went on deaf ears. She wasn't counting and wasn't sure if this was part of her points, but she hoped it was. As the flogging grew, she felt the heat rising from her sore ass cheeks.

He stopped only because he wanted to get on with her punishment. But he wanted to do one last thing. He straddled her back but didn't put his weight on her. His cock and balls rested between her shoulder blades as he encircled the instrument he used to turn her ass cheeks fire engine red, around her neck. It was a hard and thick strap forming a bit into her neck. He leaned down to her ear and spoke as he tightened his hold, cutting off her breathing, "When I return we will continue." Puppet's head floated as her lack of air supply slowly made her dizzy.

She had fallen asleep dreaming about water, she awoken trying to catch her breath. Her Master, sitting on the bed beside her, smiled down at her. He had removed the blindfold.

"You can hold your breath better when you sleep, dog; for that I will take five points off." He returned the blind fold and climbed off the bed. "Ready to cash in the rest of your points?" he didn't wait for her reply. "At your feet are five toys of punishment laid out as one, two, three, four and five. How many points do you have?"

"Fifteen, Master," she said still feeling the tingle of the beating.

"All right, choose one of the numbers."

"Five."

"Now how many points do you want me to deliver on you?"

"Five.'

"Fine," he retrieved the toy and started to rub it along her skin. It was hard, flat-surfaced, gliding across her legs, between her thighs, to her buttocks, across her back and shoulders, ending on her cheek. "Do you know what it is, cunt?" She winced, knowing her ass was going to receive another round of welts.

"A—paddle, Master," she said, her voice stuttering.

"Correct--." The first blow came across her ass cheek she cringed when the second came even harder. Her cries were drowned out by each additional blow. What were five blows felt like ten. "...next number," her Master demanded. "Hurry up or I'll add more points!"

"Four."

"Good choice, how many points?"

"Three."

"Very well," He picked up the toy and dropped them on her back. There were many of them. "What toy are these, cunt?"

"Clothes pins."

"Correct again. Now I'm going to attach many of these on your flesh, since you chose three points, I'll only keep them on for three minutes. Let's begin."

He began to work on the skin under her arms, around the sensitive area of her nipples that he had to pull from beneath her. Her ass cheeks were showed mercy and he shoved a pillow under her stomach, so he had better access between her legs. Two pins were fastened to each of her lips and one gripped her clit.

Puppet moaned in discomfort, but he didn't stop decorating her, pinning the toys in her inner thighs. He stepped away observing his work and felt pleased.

"I'm setting a timer for three minutes, you can hear it tick down starting now."

But he wasn't going to leave it at that, no he had to make it fun for him. Carefully, he ran his hands over the clothes pins sending Puppet into a frenzy of pain and pleasure.

"Please, no—Master." Her body wriggled to evade his touch but not being able to see made it difficult.

"Keep moving, if any of the pins fall off the timer starts over."

"No, Master—please I can't…"

"No, it hasn't been a minute yet and already you want me to stop? I'll tell you what, I'll stop, but you have to take five more points, is it a deal?" he played with the pins between her legs.

"Yes, yes, Master," she said in misery.

He seemed annoyed but complied as he removed the pins one by one. The blood returned to the parts that were blocked off. She whimpered as he patted her sore flesh.

"All right, let's see where you're at...You had fifteen but you won five back, which gave you ten; you betted three but backed out so you not only get that back, but also five more which leaves you with what, dog?"

"Fifteen, Master."

"Back at the beginning, select a number."

"One, Master."

"How many points, and let me remind you that whatever points you have left by the last toy will be used in full."

"Five, Master."

"Five it is." He retrieved the whip and cracked it in the air. "What toy is it dog?"

"A whip, Master."

"Correct!" he said, feeling the leather strain run across his hand and fingers.

The first blow was on her back, the second on her ass, the pain was agonizing but she couldn't speak. Another blow came across her back and the last two were on her ass and thighs. Puppet laid moaning as the pain grew to a burning numb. Her Master rubbed his pet's ass, back and thighs, feeling the heat that rose from them.

"You're at ten again, you have two toys left and I'm going to tell you what they are but not their numbers. One's a dildo and the other is a riding crop. Pick a number, two or three?"

"Two, Master."

"How many points?"

She wanted this, to be his prisoner, but either one could mean pain and only the riding crop was what she dreaded the most.

"Five, Master."

I'll make a deal with you, I'll allow you to change your choice but only if you take all ten points."

"No thank you, Master, I'll stay like this."

"Fine, open your mouth, wide."

She obeyed. He shoved the dildo in.

"Lick it, get it wet, I want it to slide into your arse."

Puppet worked faithfully getting it wet with her spit. All the while he was working her arse hole open with his fingers that he pretreated with his own spit. When he was happy with her work, he shoved it inside her at full length. He set the timer for five minutes, signifying when the dildo will be released. When it started to count, he turned a nob at the end of the fake dick and it began to vibrate. Puppet let out a deep moan as she felt the sensation grow inside her as he began to fuck her with the cock slow at first but then he quickened the pace, his free hand groping her tender arse cheeks.

Then rammed three of his digits into her hot cunt and finger fucked her hard.

She creamed his fingers again and again oh, she never wanted it to end but than that damn buzzer sounded and he ripped his fingers from her soaked pussy and the cock from her arse, causing her body to shake from the loss.

"We come to the end." He picked up the riding crop and patted it on her arse gently. She struggled for the first time, not wanting to feel the vicious sting from it.

"You're not going anywhere, cunt." He ripped the blindfold off her and leaned his cock to her mouth. She sucked it with eagerness hoping he would change his mind about using the weapon on her.

CRACK

The first blow was on her right ass cheek; her scream was muffled by his cock being pushed down her throat.

CRACK

Again nowhere to run or cry out, she struggled to move her sore arse out of his reach.

CRACK

He grabbed hold of her hair and fucked her mouth hard and fast as he ready to send down another blow.

CRACK

"One more, dog, ready or not."

CRACK

He threw the crop down and untied her wrists and ankles as he turned her onto her back and raised her legs onto his shoulders. His rigid cock, leaking of pre-cum, posed at the wet entrance mixing his cream with hers.

"You deserve this, Puppet," he said easing into her moist hole. Once he felt his balls hit her arse cheeks, his thrusting commenced into uncontrollable fucking. He bent her legs over her head as he leaned down kissing her mouth and sucking her tits. Puppet's mind and body soared to heaven as he buried his hard meat into her. Countless thrust and he rose to flip her over and made her kneel, spreading her burning cheeks apart and driving his hot, wet tongue into her arse hole sliding down to her wet clit licking savagely, sucking, biting, even his fingers showed no mercy to her willing holes as they darted in and out of the dripping cavities.

His cock was hungry; he entered her arse fucking fast and determined to bring them both over the edge, their cries blending into each other. He exploded his seed inside of her and she released her last orgasm as well. Collapsing on top of her, he remained inside her until his cock shrunk back to normal and slipped out; he fell to his side and spooned her close to his body as they both drift off to sleep.

Hours later, Puppet woke up alone; with great discomfort but with wonderful pain, she rose to go find her Master who was in the kitchen, cooking. The wonderful smell ignited the hunger pain in her stomach.

She dropped to her hands and knees and started to crawl towards him and the delectable aroma.

"Stop," he said with his back to her.

She obeyed and sat back on her heels waiting for his command.

From what she could see, he was finished cooking as he scrapped the last of his creation onto two plates.

He tossed the frying pan into the sink as he wiped his hands on a towel and carried the two meals to an eating nook that was not of her sight.

He didn't return, as Puppet waited with anticipation for his call, she could hear him talking with someone. Her heart seemed to clench in her chest as the voice was that of another woman.

"Crawl in here, Puppet," he ordered.

With glee, she obeyed and scurried to him not wanting him to wait another second for his pet. She entered and saw her Master sitting across from a female with red hair. It was cut short in a pixie style. She wore a dressing gown that touched the floor and hung free over her pale but milky shoulders, the top of her breasts crowned, not revealing what has to have been plump pink nipples.

Puppet could feel the spit in my mouth flourish as dirty, lustful, sinful thoughts possessed her mind.

They both ignored her as she sat back on her heels, not making a sound.

They chattered away in-between bites and sips of what looked like flutes filled with Champagne. Puppet watched her mouth as her lips parted to take in the substance and close, allowing the sliver to slide, dragging off its offering. She saw her peach lips lick away any remnants left behind.

How she wanted to have the honor to do that for her. Puppet turned her gaze to her Master who was refilling his flute glass and drowning half the glass. His hair was disarrayed, not combed in the way he normally wears it; it was as if someone's fingers ran through it, pulled it or claimed it, even his lips were fuller as if he was kissing someone for a long time. His neck had a passion mark that she was not allowed to give. He wore his robe like her, loose and telling.

Their meal was almost over when her Master looked at her.

"Puppet, go kneel beside my guest." Not wanting to anger him, she took her place beside the woman's chair but not for long, her hair was grab and she was pulled between the red head's legs; she wouldn't dare fight as she was positioned facing her exposed crotch, her ginger hairy crotch. She placed one leg on Puppet's shoulder and dug her heel into her back to push her forward. Puppet glanced up at her to see what she'll have her do. Her once soft green eyes now cold and demanding looked down at her, holding her flute glass, sitting back in her chair.

She spoke to her Master as she held Puppet's gaze.

"I thought you said she was trained, she seems clueless."

She was questioning her Master's word about his pet. She couldn't let him lose face, she'll lose him forever.

As if the answer came to her, she plunged her mouth into her hairy mound and snaked her tongue between her two folds; she found her wet slippery treasure and lapped at it hungrily.

Puppet felt her hips moving towards her, wanting a deeper penetration; she held her hair as Puppet grasped her yielding thighs and raised them so she could taste her wet opening. Puppet's tongue darted in and out of the dripping tunnel, tasting her scent as she increased her pleasure running her muscle up and down her trail. She cried out as Puppet felt her body shake as she squirted her cream into the hungry, welcoming mouth. Puppet drank every drop until she tugged her head away and kicked Puppet to the floor, remaining where she landed.

"Did I not tell you she was experienced?"

As she caught her breath, she looked at him and smiled.

"You were right, her tongue is wonderful. I want to fuck her."

"In due time, Puppet needs to be fed and groomed. Jessie, enter," he said calling towards the door. To Puppet's surprise, her sitter was there. "Jessie, take Puppet away and feed, bathe and ready her for entertainment for my guest."

"Yes, Mr. Utter." Jessie looked at Puppet and smiled, approaching her, Puppet raised on her knees as she fastened her leash onto her collar and quietly lead her out of the room.

Puppet's sleep was interrupted by a nudge. She fluttered her tired eyes open to stare at a familiar female that she remembered wearing worn clothes. The female gardener sat smiling back at her as Puppet took in her now, nude body. Puppet sat up and looked for her Master, but he was nowhere to be found.

"Mr. Utter is allowing us to be alone," she said, reaching out and grasping Puppet's hard nipple and pinching it between her fingers. Puppet didn't flinch from the pain but instead leaned into it.

"We are allowed to play together?" asked Puppet.

"I'm allowed to play with you."

"Then use me...what is your name?"

"My Masters call me Mia."

"You have more than one Master?"

"Two, you saw them kissing."

"Are they with my Master?"

"No more questions, Puppet." Mia pulled Puppet from the bed and walked her out the bedroom. She held her wrist in a vice grip and pulled her onto the patio. Puppet skidded to a halt when she saw the pool.

Mia looked back at her, not releasing her wrist. "Puppet, it's time for your next lesson. I'm to teach you to swim."

"No, my Master already did my lesson, its' over." She tried to tug her hand free, but Mia's grip wouldn't budge. "Let go or I'll tell."

"Tell who?"

"Puppet," Troy's voice echoed in her ears as Puppet looked behind her and saw him standing there.

Still unable to break free from Mia, Puppet twisted her body towards Troy.

"Master, please, she's trying to make me go into the pool again."

Troy walked up to them and Mia released Puppet's wrist, who in turn rushed to her Master. Troy made her face him gaining her full attention.

"It's time you learn to swim, Puppet. And I arranged Mia to come over and teach you, her Master informed me she was a talented swimmer and I feel you will be in capable hands. Isn't that right, Mia?"

"Yes, Master Troy." Puppet looked back and saw that Mia had dropped to her knees and bowed her head.

"Very good, Mia. Now, Puppet, you are to do exactly what Mia instructs and if you try to flee or whine your way out, I will whip you until you pass out, understood?"

"Yes, Master."

"Mia, take Puppet to her lesson." Mia rose to her feet and reached out for Puppet's hand, who willingly gave it over. Without a glance back, knowing her Master would be angered, Puppet accepted her fate.

Puppet stood by the edge of the pool and stared at the water; it still looked intimidating and her heart raced at the thought of climbing back in it. She watched Mia, who, after releasing her hand, walked alone to the far end where the deepest part of the pool was and waved at Puppet just before diving in head first. Puppet held her breath as Mia swam part of the way before surfacing for air, her head bobbed before disappearing again. She looked down and saw the way the water made Mia's body seem to bend at places. She surfaced right below Puppet, smiling at her. Come in, Puppet, you will love this lesson. Puppet wanted to enjoy Mia's body but had no choice but to follow.

She sat down and slowly slipped into the pool and held on to the side until her feet touched the bottom then faced Mia. '"Now give me your hands." Puppet placed her palm in Mia's, who moved them to her shoulders. "Now, I want you to hold my shoulders and don't let go until I tell you okay?"

"What are you going to do?"

"I'm going to swim to the middle of the pool in the deep end with you floating on top of me."

"What—no, please…?" Puppet tried to pull way, but again Mia trapped her wrist in an unbreakable hold.

"Puppet," she turned and her Master stared down at her. "You're going to do this because I told you to." She hesitated, her response was to bite her lip and look downward. Her Master's silence burned into her, she knew he wasn't going to repeat himself as she turned to Mia and placed her hands in her shoulders. Mia smiled, but she wasn't making eye contact with Puppet. Only before she opened her mouth to talk, Mia propelled herself back, taking Puppet with her.

Their breast merged as Mia held Puppet above the water using her body as a floatation device. Puppet tightened her grasp which will leave a lasting impression on Mia's skin, but as they sail to the middle of the pool, Mia became relax as she felt weightless.

"Okay, Puppet, I want you to do what I do." Puppet watched as Mia outstretched her arms like wings, caressing the rippling water using the wave to move her body. It took several tries but Puppet developed a routine that she never thought she knew. For every accomplished move Puppet made, she was rewarded with a lip sucking kiss from Mia. Puppet wanted to be rewarded, so she paid close attention to her acting teacher and followed her every command, forgetting her fear of sinking. The first reward was only lips, as in a peck, then gradually it became lips with tongue. Mia even gave Puppet a treat, unaware to Master Troy as he lounged on his back, jerking his cock slowly in his fist.

A tender touch with her fingers between Puppet's legs, grazing the skin along her thighs, then moving to the hairless mound that Puppet parted her legs for; Mia felt the wetness from the pool water but also a sensual dampness that she ran her digits through, grasping the firm clit between her fingers and squeezing it. Puppet suppressed her cries from the delightful sensation as she kissed Mia deeply, wrapping one's tongue around the other.

Her lesson continued until Master Troy looked over.

"Enough for now, Puppet, I want you here."

It was not for debate as Puppet swam over to where her Master was and climbed out of the pool. She approached him, dropping to her knees and bowing her head. She didn't notice Mia swimming the other way climbing out and leaving them alone.

Puppet had hoped she and Mia could pleasure her Master, but she wasn't going to bring that up as she sensed her Master was in a good mood.

"Come suck my cock while I talk to you."

Still dripping wet, she crawled to him and straddled him with her head pointed at his feet and her ass displayed for his pleasure. His cock rested on his stomach as she licked the head, waking it up as it rose for her; then moistening her mouth first, she took the healthy muscle into her hot mouth, stopping half-way then slowly pulled back. She swallowed again and this time she made it to the base of his cock, feeling it touch the back of her throat. Her head began to bob up and down as she ran her tongue along his stiff, veiny shaft.

"I have to say I am very proud of you. You were amazing out there." She started to raise her head to thank him, but he pushed her on her back, signaling her not to stop. "How I wanted to fuck you both with my fist until you creamed all over my cock. But Mia belongs to someone else and she was only called to teach you to swim." He stopped speaking as he felt his body tingle from the pet's tongue. He grasped her ass and squeezed both cheeks digging his nails into her flesh. If he wanted to, he could break her skin but not today. He wanted to fire down her throat his hot climax. He wanted to hear her take deep swallows of his seed until he was empty; He wanted to ram his fingers inside, which would send her body over the edge, but didn't because as far as he was concerned, she didn't deserve it.

Puppet's mouth stroked her Master's tool as her hands massaged his balls every so often, moving her mouth to the sack, sucking each nut until they were drenched while she gave him a hand job.

She felt his sack grow in her mouth as she hurried back to his cock and buried it down her throat. Occasionally, she felt a hard slap on one or both of her arse cheeks as she listened to her Master moan his delight. He thrust his pelvis upward, sending his cock deeper down her throat, fucking her mouth hard and fast. He exploded as he hoped, buried in her throat. His body shook from his orgasm as he slowly came down from his high and laid motionless on the lounge chair. Puppet kept sucking until she was sure he was dry and clean. She looked back and waited for his command, but none came, in fact, to her he looked like he fell asleep.

She wasn't sure what to do, she was still wet and didn't want to make him uncomfortable, so she decide to climb off. As she raised her leg, she felt his strong hand clutch her ankle tightly.

"Did I say you could get down, cunt?" he pushed her off of him and Puppet smacked the hard tile floor. She scrambled to her knees and put her head down. Master Troy rose and walked away, Puppet kept her eyes down not daring to follow him with her gaze. He returned with her leash and fastened it on her collar. He tugged hard, bringing her head up and making her look at him.

"You never listen, you always want to defy me."

"No, Master."

"Shut up, you are not to say a word. You think I didn't know Mia was playing with my property, or when you didn't follow my command about getting in that water? I never said you two could kiss and you sure as hell didn't ask my permission. You need more training and I think it's time I send you back to get it." Puppet shook with fear at the thought of seeing Michael again. "Now, now, Puppet, don't you want to see where I sent Jessie? You are going to be made an example for old and new pets."

He tugged on her leash and made her follow him back into the house. Puppet heard faint cries from one of the rooms as she was lead on her knees towards a door; her Master knocked once before it opene. Puppet was shocked to see Mia, hands and feet bound with leather and mouth gagged, lying on the floor. She was being whipped with a cat of nine tails by the nude young male who Puppet saw from her bedroom window kissing the older gardener. The red welts were very visible on Mia, who looked over at Puppet with not tears in her eyes but lust. Puppet trembled with burning delight as her Master exchanged words with the gardener, whom Puppet didn't see right away, but was delighted to see him naked, wearing only a jock strap without a cup and a pair of leather biker boots.

"Let's go, Puppet, it's time to arrange your trip." Before she knew it, the door closed with a bang and she was taken from the house where Master Troy's driver was waiting with the trunk open. Her Master made her crawl over the grass until they reached the car and he dropped her leash into the hand of the driver who grabbed Puppet by the collar, lifted her off the ground and tossed her into the trunk. Removing the leash, he made her turn over as he tied her wrists and ankles latching both together and strapping a thick gag ball around her mouth, slamming the trunk door closed.

He climbed into the driver's seat and looked back at his employer for instructions.

"Is my jet ready?"

"Yes, sir, and I informed them that you were coming with a drop off."

"Good, then let's not keep Michael waiting."

Puppet was jerked around as she felt the car moving.

"Poor, Jessie," she thought. "So that's where you disappeared to." To think, Michael had his own sick way, which makes Puppet wet and tingle with anticipation.

THE END

Here is a sample from another story you may enjoy:

HOT SUBMISSIVE ROMANCE

Puppet Master

Pet Sitting, Book 2

D.D. Watson

Puppet found one movie ticket and a note from her Master telling her to get dressed, take a cab to the theater he provided an address for, and to meet him outside at 11p.m. tonight.

Springing to her feet, Puppet raced upstairs and into her room, opening her walk-in closet. She knew what she was going to wear and wasted no time getting herself pampered and noticeable for her Master.

Fourteen days she was without him. Sure, Jessie's wet clit was mouthwatering and velvety and her breasts were firm and those nipples bitable. Puppet could still feel Jessie's wet tongue lapping at her anus most keenly, then adding her many fingers to bring her over the edge with great force that she almost repeated her climax just thinking about it. But she needed her Master.

Puppet regained control and called for a cab, just as her Master instructed. She used the cell phone he had given her a month ago. The cab arrived and when the driver saw her, he hopped out of the cab and opened her door for her.

She arrived, finding herself in front of an adult movie theater.

"Are you sure this is here you want to go, Miss?" asked the cab driver, who seemed concerned for her wellbeing.

She looked at him without a hint of doubt and smiled. "I'm meeting a friend who will take care of me, thank you."

He slowly pulled off, but then received a call for his dispatch about another fare. He then seemed to forget about her and sped off.

She looked at her ticket, which only had the name of the theater on it, wondering if she were to go inside.

Several different men walked into the theater glancing at her as they passed through the blacked out doors.

She started to back away thinking it would be best to wait down the street when her cell phone went off. She jumped from the vibration in her pocket and answered it right away.

"Hello," she said.

"Are you out there, whore?" It was her Master's commanding voice. A smile washed over her face. Just hearing him ignited the heat between her legs.

"Yes, Master."

"Are you facing the theater?"

"Yes, Master."

"Then come in and find me, the usher will tell you which theater I'm in."

Still having not seen one woman go in caused her some anxiety.

"Master, can you stay on the phone with me until I find you-" The line went dead.

She had a feeling he would do that. She returned her phone to her pocket and swallowed her fears and entered the forbidden place.

The usher leered long and hard, she could have sworn she saw him nod at someone. She handed him her ticket and he directed her to theater one.

When she entered, the heavy door shut quickly behind her. The movie was already playing and it was too dark for her to see anyone or even a seat.

The film showed a woman being ravished by three men. One fucked her in the ass, another used her clit and the third worked her mouth. Her hands were tied behind her back and a belt was around her neck. The one who was fucking her ass was pulling on the leather as he tore into her backside.

Puppet was getting wet and aroused from watching it. Her eyesight adjusted so she started down the aisle searching for her tolerant Master.

She was almost to the front of the theater when a hand reached out and grabbed her arm, pulling her into a row of seats. She wanted to scream but was silenced with a hot mouth covering hers.

Puppet melted into the kiss that was warm and strong. His tongue searched her mouth with great hunger. His hand snaked around her neck, holding her jaw in place as he deepened their kiss. Puppet was losing herself in the burning embrace when she realized she didn't know whom she was kissing.

She wasn't going to betray her Master at a Burlesque movie with someone she couldn't see. She tried to break free from his lips when she felt two hands from behind groping her breasts, kneading them like clay. Her nipples were squeezed and pulled through her dress. She tried to fend them off but it was so intoxicating she didn't want it to stop. She was so weak…so wet and in need of relief.

The kiss was broken and Puppet was left breathless, her head, spinning from the contact. The hands that were fondling her tits pulled her back into the aisle and threw her to the floor.

She staggered to her feet and moved quickly down front.

Still trying to search for her Master proved to be difficult when someone came from behind and grasped her waist, grinding his midsection that was protruding a healthy hard cock into her Master's property.

Puppet tried to stop his advances when she saw him, her Master, approaching. He took her wrists into his hands and lowered them to her side.

"Obey Puppet," he said, "Obey."

Puppet relaxed and allowed the stranger to undo her dress…

If you enjoyed this sample then look for **Puppet Master.**

Also by this Author

Train Wreck

Pet Sitting

Puppet Master

About the Author

D.D. Watson is an up and coming writer of short stories and novels.

Born on June 24th under the cancer moon, D.D. Watson develops the taste for reading and writing at a young age.

"I love the naked body and creating wonderful stories about them. Traveling is my passion and I plan on going around the world."

D.D. Watson spent every day learning the skill of writing.

From the Author

Check my page on Amazon and my blog for Updates and interesting info.

Author Central - http://www.amazon.com/D.D.-Watson/e/B00FF605LI

If you enjoyed any of my books then please share the love and click like on my books in Amazon.

If you write me a review and send me an email I will send you a free book, or many.
(Just know that these emails are filtered by my publisher.)

Good news is always welcome.

One Last Thing, For Kindle Readers...

When you turn the page, Kindle will give you the opportunity to rate this book and share your thoughts on Facebook and Twitter. If you enjoyed my writings, would you please take a few seconds to let your friends know about it? Because... when they enjoy they will be grateful to you and so will I.

Thank You!

D. D. Watson
dd_watson@awesomeauthors.org